Sukey
and the
Mermaid

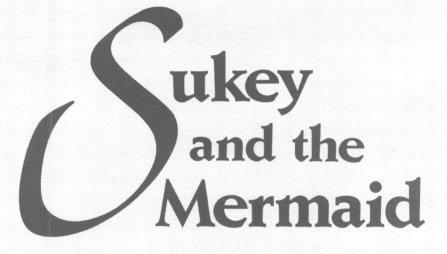

ROBERT D. SAN SOUCI
ILLUSTRATED BY BRIAN PINKNEY

FOUR WINDS PRESS ❖ NEW YORK

MAXWELL MACMILLAN CANADA   TORONTO   MAXWELL MACMILLAN INTERNATIONAL   NEW YORK   OXFORD   SINGAPORE   SYDNEY

Four Winds Press   Maxwell Macmillan Canada, Inc.
Macmillan Publishing Company   1200 Eglinton Avenue East
866 Third Avenue   Suite 200
New York, NY 10022   Don Mills, Ontario M3C 3N1

Macmillan Publishing Company is part of the
Maxwell Communication Group of Companies.

FIRST AMERICAN EDITION
Printed and bound in the United States of America
10   9   8   7   6   5   4   3   2   1

The text of this book is set in Weiss Bold.
Book design by Christy Hale

Library of Congress Cataloging-in-Publication Data
San Souci, Robert D.
Sukey and the mermaid / Robert D. San Souci ; illustrated by Brian
Pinkney. — 1st American ed.
p.   cm.
Summary: Unhappy with her life at home, Sukey receives kindness
and wealth from Mama Jo the mermaid.
ISBN 0-02-778141-0
[1. Mermaids.   2. Folklore, Afro-American.]   I. Pinkney, Brian,
ill.   II. Title.
PZ8.1.S227Su   1992
398.21—dc20
[E]   90-24559

A NOTE FROM THE ARTIST

The work in this book was done in scratchboard and oil
pastels. Scratchboard is a technique that requires a white
board to be covered with black ink. The ink is "scratched"
off with a sharp tool to reveal the white underneath. Color
is then added with oil pastels. The oil pastels are rubbed
into the "scratched" lines and the excess is wiped away
with Liquin. I like this way of working because it allows
me to sculpt as well as draw the images.

For Barbara S. Kouts
Agent, friend, and sometime guardian angel
extraordinaire   —R.S.S.

To my sisters-in-law,
Sandra, Kimm, and Lynne   —B.P.

Storyteller say,
This happened oncet upon a time,
on a little island off the coast
of South Carolina.

A GIRL NAMED SUKEY lived with her ma and step-pa in a cabin with a sagging porch and a roof so rickety it let in sunshine or rain, depending on the weather. Every morning at day-clean, Sukey would get up to sling her hoe at the weeds in the vegetable garden. If she stopped to fan herself with her wide straw hat, her step-pa would shout, "Sukey, don't you be skylarking!"

The girl's mother called her new husband "Mister Jones," but Sukey had her own name for the bossy, do-nothing man. As her hoe rose and fell, she sang,

> "Mister Hard-Times,
>   Since you come
>   My ma don't like me,
>   My work never done.
>
> "Mister Hard-Times
>   Won't do a lick,
>   Just say, 'Work faster
>   Or whip you with a stick.' "

One hot afternoon, when her step-pa wasn't looking, Sukey threw down her hoe and took off. She ran through the woods of pine and palmetto and mossy oak, past dunes fringed with broom grass, to the beach of shining white sand that was her secret hideaway.

She sat down, pulled off her hat, and unwound the white kerchief from around her head. The sea breeze cooled her burning face while she wriggled her bare feet deep to where the sand was wet and cold.

She sang a little song she had heard somewhere:

"Thee, thee, down below,
Come to me, Mama Jo!"

Suddenly, a beautiful, brown-skinned, black-eyed mermaid rose up in the water. Hair as green as seaweed hung down to the mermaid's waist. Sunlight sparked off the gold combs in her hair and the green scales of her fishtail.

The girl was mighty frightened, but the mermaid said pleasantly, "How do, my lady. You look so hot there in the sun. Come into the water and cool off."

No   Sukey had heard folks warn, "Them mermans cotch you and pull you beneath the water." So she said, "No, missus, I can't swim."

"I'll teach you to swim, if you wish," the mermaid said. Then she added, gently, "You have no reason to fear me, my lady. I came because your song called me."

But Sukey would only wade along the water's edge while the mermaid dove under the waves and rose and dove again. Each time she brought Sukey something: a curious shell, or red and white coral, or bits of green and blue glass polished like jewels by the sea.

When the sun began to set, Sukey cried, "Oh, I'm gonna be whipped for sure. I clean forgot to feed the chickens and draw water from the river."

"Give this to your folks," said the mermaid, pressing a gold coin into Sukey's hand, "and they won't scold you. But you must promise not to tell them about me. When you want to see me again, just come here and sing:

'Thee, thee, down below,
Come to me, Mama Jo!' "

Then Mama Jo disappeared beneath the waves.

Sukey hurried home. At first her ma and step-pa yelled because she had not done her chores. But when she gave them the mermaid's coin, they stared in wonder.

"Where'd you get this?" her ma asked.

"On the edge of the water," said Sukey.

"Well," said her step-pa, "go off tomorrow to the water edge, and see can you find some more of these."

"I will," Sukey answered, happy to have more time to spend with the mermaid.

AFTER THIS, Sukey went to the shore every morning when the day was clean. The mermaid taught her to swim, and sometimes they dove through the water together. One day, the two sat talking beside the waves.

"Soon I'm gonna leave this island and go over to the main," said Sukey. "I'll live in a fine place like Beaufort or Charleston."

"My home is below the sea, away from the world of men," said Mama Jo. "You could come with me, if you want."

"I don't think so," said Sukey.

Before she dove under the waves at first dark, the mermaid would give Sukey one small gold coin. This the girl gave to her folks, so her ma could buy meat and rice and flannel. But Mister Jones spent most on *malafee*, whiskey that came by boat from the mainland. So things were not much better in the tumbledown cabin.

Sukey's ma grew more and more curious to know where her daughter found the gold coins. One morning, she followed Sukey to the shore. Hiding in the broom grass on a sand dune, she heard Sukey sing:

"Thee, thee, down below,
Come to me, Mama Jo!"

The woman watched in amazement as the girl and mermaid swam in the ocean. And she saw the mermaid give Sukey one gold coin at day's end.

That night, while Sukey slept, her ma whispered to Mister Jones about what she had seen.

"If I cotch that merman," her husband said, "I'll sell'm on the main for a pile of gold."

Before Day-Clean, as Sukey was sleeping, her ma and step-pa carried their canoe down to the shore. There the woman sang:

"Thee, thee, down below,
Come to me, Mama Jo!"

When the mermaid rose up in the water, Mister Jones chased her in the canoe. He flung his net at her, but the angry mermaid dove beneath the water. She did not come up again, though Sukey's ma sang the magic song over and over. At last, husband and wife gave up and went home, each blaming the other for what had happened.

They said nothing to Sukey, who went to the shore as usual.

But Mama Jo did not answer the girl's song that day, or any day. Sukey grieved for her lost friend. Because there was no more gold, Mister Jones made her hoe the garden, clean the house, and haul water until she took sick.

Soon she grew so weak that she could barely get out of bed. But, in a dream, the mermaid visited her and said, "I will come to you once more, and take you to live with me beneath the sea. If you want this, go to the shore, and sing:

'Thee, thee, down below,
Take me down, Mama Jo!' "

Though she was very tired and sickly, Sukey crept down to the shore while her ma and step-pa were away. There she sang softly:

"Thee, thee, down below,
Take me down, Mama Jo!"

To her joy, the mermaid rose up. She wrapped strands of her magical hair around Sukey, so the girl could travel safely beneath the waves. Then they plunged into the ocean.

The mermaid carried Sukey down, down through the water to her home in the seawall. Sukey found herself in a vast, dry cave. All around her, mother-of-pearl glowed and filled the place with soft, warm light.

Mama Jo said, "This is your home now. I will never scold you down here."

FOR A WHILE, Sukey was happy. The mermaid taught her sea songs and gave her strands of pearls and showed her a rusty chest filled with gold and jewels from a sunken pirate ship. In return, Sukey would amuse her friend with riddles she had learned.

But after some length of time, the girl began to pine for the sound of human voices and the mockingbird's sweet song at day-clean, for the scent of wild magnolias and jasmine, for the sky of delicious blue, dotted with white clouds and gulls.

She pleaded with Mama Jo, "Do carry me back home, missus."

At first the mermaid said no. But, touched by Sukey's tears, she said, "Very well. If you ask me a riddle I can't answer, I will take you home."

So Sukey thought and thought. Finally, she said, "There's something that walk all day and when night come, she go under the bed and rest. What's that?"

Mama Jo thought and thought, but she could not solve the riddle.

"That's a *shoe*!" Sukey cried. She had picked the riddle because the mermaid had no feet, and Sukey was always barefoot.

"I will carry you back to land," said Mama Jo with a sigh. "But time has passed in the world above while you have been with me. You are a grown woman now. Go to the pirate's chest and take a bagful of coins and jewels. This will be your dowry. When you return, many men will court you, but marry only the man named Dembo. If you choose another husband, your treasure will disappear."

THEN THE MERMAID wrapped her mossy hair around Sukey and brought her to shore. The young woman returned to the rickety cabin, where she found her ma and step-pa. Sukey's ma had grown old grieving for her lost daughter; she embraced Sukey with tears of joy.

Mister Jones had just grown meaner, until he seemed only dry bones and bitterness. Seeing Sukey's treasure, he pretended to welcome her home. He hid his face in his hands as though he were crying, too, but he couldn't squeeze one salt tear from his eyes.

When the story got around that the young woman had brought a rich dowry, all the young men came courting her. But Sukey remembered the mermaid's warning and refused them all. Then, one day, a hardworking fisherman rowed across from the mainland to court her. "Name is Dembo," he said simply.

Sukey studied his eyes and saw love and honesty and kindness in them. Though he was not as tall or as handsome as her other suitors, she was happy with the man the mermaid had chosen for her.

Sukey's ma and her neighbors planned a fine wedding. But Mister Jones had other plans. "I'm gonna get that gold," he promised himself.

The night before the wedding, while Sukey and her ma were away, the wicked man struck Dembo dead and stole the treasure. No one saw him do the deed, so he hid the bag under his mattress.

When Sukey discovered the crime, her grief was beyond measure. She ran to the seashore, where she cried:

"Thee, thee, down below,
Come to me, Mama Jo!"

The mermaid appeared, and Sukey told her unhappy tale. Then Mama Jo said, "This is the last time I will come to you. My lady, you must now choose forever between my world and the world of men. Think carefully: below the sea is a gentle place without time or pain. Up here, hurt and hunger are never far away, and time is always ready to steal what little you have."

But Sukey said, "I must have Dembo. Do bring my sweetheart back to me, and I won't bother you after this."

Mama Jo dropped a seed pearl into the young woman's palm. "Set this on Dembo's lips," she told Sukey. Then, with a sad "Good-bye, my lady," she vanished beneath the waves.

SUKEY RACED BACK to her cabin, where Dembo rested in a plain pine coffin. While her ma and the other mourners looked on, she put the tiny pearl on Dembo's closed lips.

Right away life came into him again. Sitting up, he pointed to Mister Jones and cried, "That's the one who hit me!" But the wicked man snatched the treasure bag and fled to the shore, pursued by Sukey, Dembo, and the others.

Mister Jones jumped into his canoe and paddled away, but as everyone watched, a single dark cloud formed above the boat. Lightning flashed and

thunder roared. The ocean beneath the cloud began to churn, and high waves swamped the canoe. In a moment, the angry water swallowed the boat and its passenger.

Suddenly, the sky cleared and the sea calmed.

Though they were sorry to have lost the mermaid's treasure, Sukey and Dembo were happy to have each other. They comforted Sukey's ma, who said, "Mister Jones wasn't much, but he was all I had in this world."

"You got us, ma," said Sukey, giving her a hug. "We'll all be getting along just fine now."

The next day, the wedding went ahead as planned. Afterward, Sukey took Dembo's hand and led him down to the shore. As the two sat on the beach, Sukey wriggled her toes deep in the white sand and felt something hidden there. Together, they dug up the lost treasure bag.

At that moment, Sukey saw the flash of sunlight on green scales and gold combs far out to sea. She blew a kiss across the waves and heard sweet laughter in return.

Storyteller say,
I step on a thing, and the thing bend
And that's the way my story end.

AUTHOR'S NOTE

The basis of *Sukey and the Mermaid* is a brief folktale (almost a fragment) recorded in Elsie Clews Parsons's *Folk-Lore of the Sea Islands, South Carolina*, published in 1923 by the American Folk-Lore Society. It is one of the relatively few authenticated African-American folktales involving mermaids. Others can be found in Richard M. Dorson's *American Negro Folktales* and in Harold Courlander's *A Treasury of Afro-American Folklore*.

Because the Sea Island account seemed to be a brief version of a longer story, I searched for more complete narratives in other African-American traditions. This led me to investigate Caribbean folklore, where I discovered that the "Pretty Jo" of the Parsons story, or "Mama Jo" as the character is called in parallel texts, is derived from "Mama Dlo" ("Mama de l' eau" or "Water Mother," a term for mermaid). I did not find the "root tale" I sought, but many clues pointed to Africa as the likely source of a still-earlier version.

Indeed, a West African tale of a young girl's encounter with a female water-spirit provided the missing story elements for my version. With all these things in place, *Sukey and the Mermaid* began to take its present shape.